The Three Billy Goats Gruff

Retold by Rebecca Hu-Van Wright

Illustrated by Ying-Hwa Hu

STAR BRIGHT BOOKS
Cambridge, Massachusetts

To Caedmon
    –Ying-Hwa

Published in the United States of America by Star Bright Books, Inc.
The name Star Bright Books and the Star Bright Books logo are registered
trademarks of Star Bright Books, Inc.
Please visit: www.starbrightbooks.com. For bulk orders, please email:
orders@starbrightbooks.com, or call customer service at: (617) 354-1300.

Hardback ISBN-13: 978-1-59572-666-7
Paperback ISBN-13: 978-1-59572-667-4
Star Bright Books / MA / 00104140
Printed in China (WKT) 10 9 8 7 6 5 4 3 2 1

Printed on paper from sustainable forests and a percentage of
post-consumer paper.

Hu-Van Wright, Rebecca.
 The three billy goats gruff / by Rebecca Hu-Van Wright; illustrated by Ying-Hwa Hu.
    pages cm
 Summary: Three clever billy goats outwit a big, ugly troll that lives under the bridge
they must cross on their way to a greener hillside.
 ISBN 978-1-59572-666-7 (hardcover) — ISBN 978-1-59572-667-4 (pbk.)
[1. Fairy tales. 2. Folklore—Norway.] I. Hu, Ying-Hwa, illustrator. II. Asbjørnsen, Peter
Christen, 1812-1885. Tre bukkene Bruse. English. III. Title.
PZ8.H855Thr 2014
398.2--dc23
[E]
                                2013049694

Once upon a time,
there were three goats.

A big goat,

a middle-sized goat,

and a little goat.

They were called the
Three Billy Goats Gruff.

All day long they played on the hillside, eating the green grass. But there was never enough grass for the three of them, and they were always hungry.

One day, on a hill across the valley, they saw the greenest, most delicious-looking grass.

"Let us go there!" said the littlest goat, skipping about.

"I agree!" said the middle-sized goat, jumping up and down.

"Absolutely!" said the biggest goat, prancing to and fro.

"I'll go first," said the littlest goat.
"All right," agreed his brothers.

So the littlest goat headed down
the hill, through the woods,

until he came to a bridge.

"Trip, trap, trip, trap!" He trotted onto the bridge. Then he heard a thunderous voice. "WHO'S THAT CROSSING MY BRIDGE?"

The littlest goat nearly jumped out of his skin!
"It's me, the littlest Billy Goat Gruff," he said,
shaking. And out from under the bridge came
the biggest, meanest-looking Troll.

"I AM GOING TO GOBBLE YOU UP!"
he roared.

"Oh, no! Not me," said the littlest goat,
"I am too little. But my brother is coming soon,
and he's so much bigger."

The Troll thought about it. "WELL, YOU HAD BETTER BE RIGHT!" he said.

The littlest goat ran across the bridge as fast as he could go.

Next came the middle-sized Billy Goat Gruff. "Trap, trop, trap, trop!" He trotted onto the bridge. Then he heard a thunderous voice. "WHO'S THAT CROSSING MY BRIDGE?" roared the Troll. "I AM GOING TO GOBBLE YOU UP!"

"Oh, no! Not me," said the middle-sized goat.
"I'm much too small. My brother is coming soon,
and he's a lot bigger than I am."

The Troll thought about it. "WELL, YOU HAD BETTER BE RIGHT!" he said.

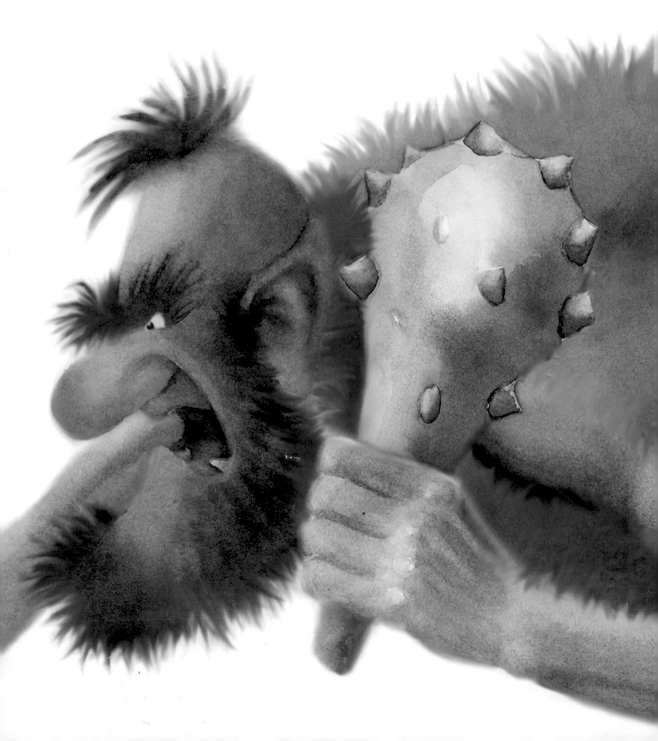

The middle-sized goat ran across the bridge as fast as he could.

Next came the biggest Billy Goat Gruff. "Trop, tramp, trop, tramp!" He trotted onto the bridge.

Then he heard a thunderous voice.
"WHO'S THAT CROSSING MY BRIDGE?"
roared the Troll. "I AM GOING TO GOBBLE
YOU UP!"

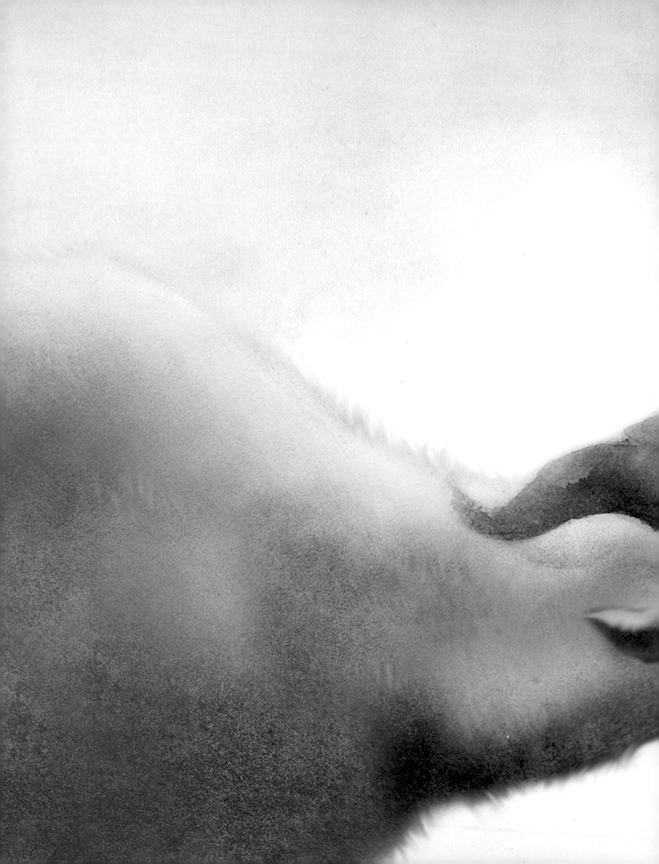

But then the Troll saw that this goat was much,
MUCH bigger than the other two goats.

He was HUGE!

And with a flick of his head, the biggest
Billy Goat Gruff butted the Troll.

SPLASH! He landed into the water below.

At last, the Three Billy Goats Gruff were together on the green grassy hillside.

There they ate the juicy grass until their
stomachs were full. And they never saw
the mean Troll again.